For Dewi Watkins,
who listened to me telling stories
on October 13, 2008
S.G.

For Jasper
J.B.

ORCHARD BOOKS
338 Euston Road, London NW1 3BH
Orchard Books Australia
Hachette Children's Books
Level 17/207 Kent Street, Sydney NSW 2000

First published by Orchard Books in 2009
First paperback publication in 2010

Text © Sally Grindley 2009
Illustrations © Jo Brown 2009

The rights of Sally Grindley to be identified as the author and
Jo Brown to be identified as the illustrator of this work
have been asserted by them in accordance with the
Copyright, Designs and Patents Act, 1988.

A CIP catalogue record for this book is available from the British Library.
All rights reserved.

ISBN 978 1 84616 153 7 (hardback)
ISBN 978 1 84616 161 2 (paperback)

1 3 5 7 9 10 8 6 4 2 (hardback)
1 3 5 7 9 10 8 6 4 2 (paperback)

Printed in China

Orchard Books is a division of Hachette Children's Books,
an Hachette UK company.

www.hachette.co.uk

THE BEAR DETECTIVES

The Ghost Train

Written by **SALLY GRINDLEY**
Illustrated by **JO BROWN**

ORCHARD BOOKS

Constable Tiggs

Sergeant Bumble

Charlie

Charlie's mother

"It's the village fair today," said
Sergeant Bumble one morning.

"Can we go on the rides?" asked
Constable Tiggs excitedly.
"We shall be too busy being
detectives," said Bumble sternly.

They walked out onto the green, which was crowded with villagers. "Steady there," said Sergeant Bumble to a young bear who nearly knocked him over.

"Say sorry to Mr Bumble,
Charlie," said the bear's mother.
"Sorry, Mr Bumble," said Charlie.

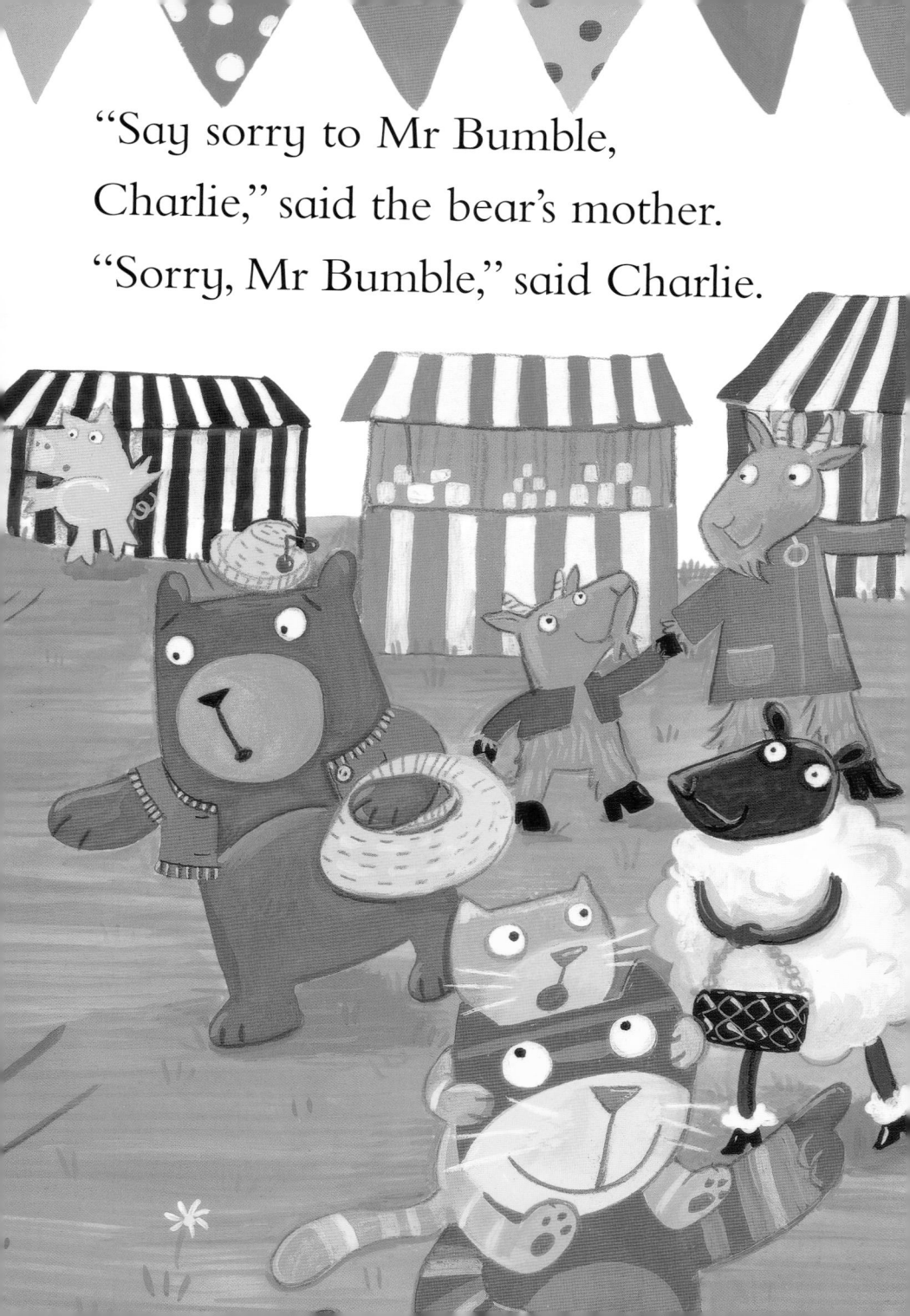

"Are you going on any of the rides?" asked Charlie.

"I'm afraid we have more important things to do," said Bumble.

"Poor Mr Bumble," said Charlie as
he skipped away, his mother trying
to keep up with him.

9

"I wish we could go on the bumper cars," said Tiggs. "We've got a car of our own," said Bumble.

They passed the whirling teacups.
"They look fun," said Tiggs.
"A cup of tea would be better,"
said Bumble.

11

When they came to the big wheel,
Bumble stood underneath and
said, "Of course, you would have
to be silly to go on that."

They had just reached the cake
stall, when they heard a loud cry.

Charlie's mother came
rushing over to them.
"Oh, Mr Bumble," she sobbed.
"It's my Charlie, I can't find
him anywhere!"

"Where did you last see him?"
asked Bumble.
"We were watching the duck race,
and when I looked round
he had gone."

"Don't worry, madam. My young
constable and I will soon find him."

"He's wearing a red hat," said Tiggs.
"If we go up on the big wheel, we
should be able to spot him."

Bumble looked horrified. "We're
not – I don't – I mean it's a long
way up there," he stuttered.

"Come on, Sir," said Tiggs.
"There's no time to lose."
Tiggs grabbed his hand,
pulled him over to the big
wheel and pushed him into
an open pod.

"Up we go!" Tiggs
shouted to the operator.

The wheel began to turn.
Up and up they went.
Bumble closed
his eyes tight.

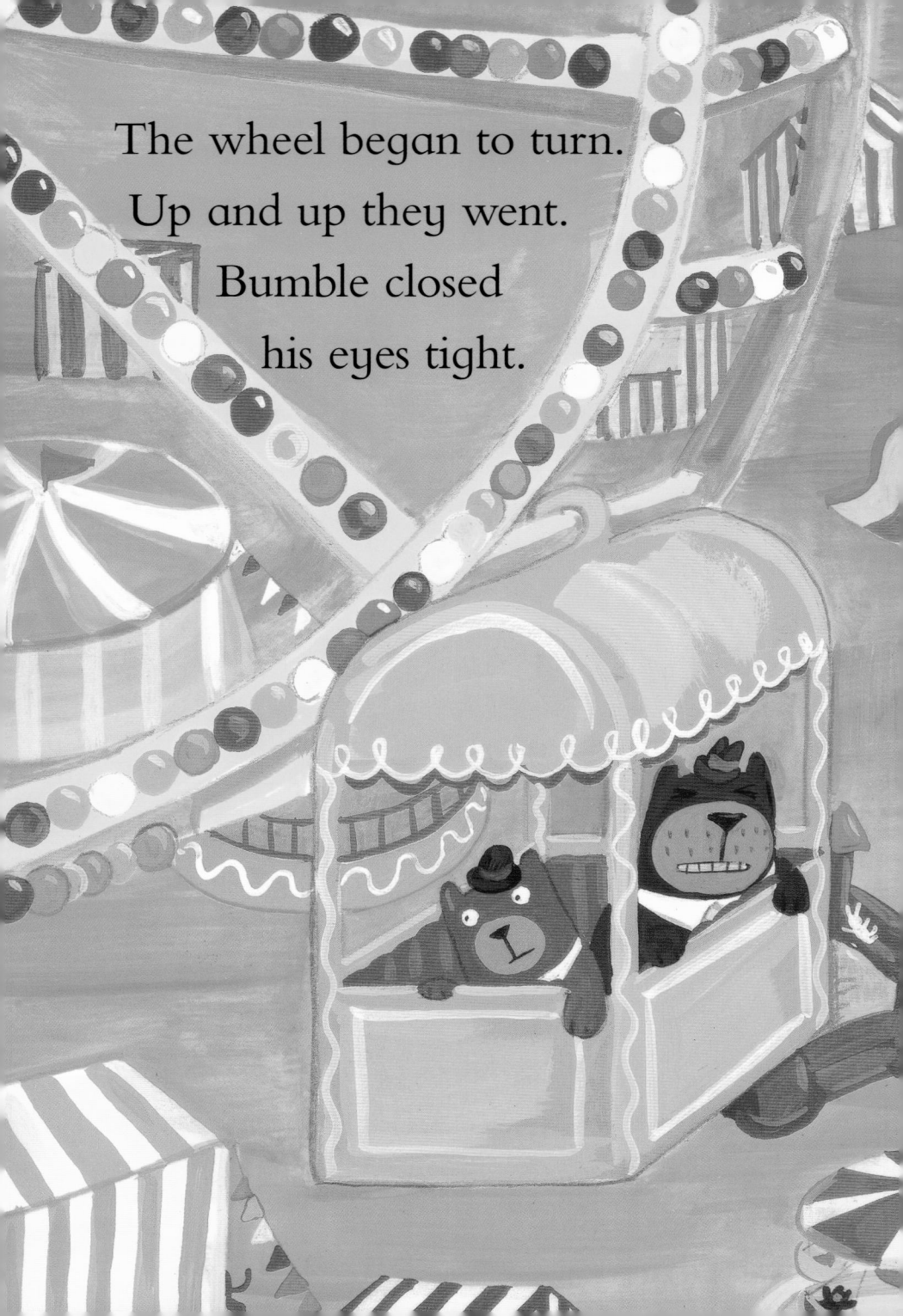

"The view's fantastic, Sir," said
Tiggs. Then suddenly he cried,
"I can see Charlie, Sir!"

"Keep an eye on him
then," Bumble groaned.

As soon as the pod reached the ground, Tiggs leapt off. Bumble stumbled behind him.

"He's heading for that tent over there," Tiggs called.

They ran after him into the tent.

It was full of mirrors. "Hey, look at
me," chuckled Tiggs, standing in
front of one of them. "I'm really tall."

"I'm not that fat!" protested
Bumble when he saw himself in
one mirror.

They couldn't find Charlie
anywhere, but when they
went outside again, Tiggs
spotted him heading
for the ghost train.

"Not the ghost train,"
groaned Bumble.

They arrived just in time to jump
into the last wagon.
"Full steam ahead!" called
the driver.

A spider's web brushed against Bumble's face. "Aargh!" he yelled.

A ghost swooped in front of him. "Eeek!" he screamed.

A skeleton jabbed a finger in his belly. "Get me out of here!" he bellowed.

"It's all right, Sir," said Tiggs.
"They're not real."
The train came back out into the
light. Standing on the platform
were Charlie and his mother.

"Now, Charlie, say sorry to
Mr Bumble for all the trouble
you've caused," Charlie's mother
said gently.

"Sorry, Mr Bumble," said Charlie.
"Have you had a nice day?"
"Ha, yes, of course," blustered Bumble.
"Now, try not to get lost again."

29

Charlie skipped away,
his mother still trying
to keep up with him.

"Well, Constable Tiggs," said Bumble, "after our fine piece of detective work, I think we've had enough of fairs for one day, don't you?"

"Yes, Sir," smiled Tiggs. "I'll make you a nice cup of tea."

THE BEAR DETECTIVES

SALLY GRINDLEY 🎩 JO BROWN

Bucket Rescue	978 1 84616 152 0
Who Shouted Boo?	978 1 84616 109 4
The Ghost Train	978 1 84616 153 7
Treasure Hunt	978 1 84616 108 7
The Mysterious Earth	978 1 84616 155 1
The Strange Pawprint	978 1 84616 156 8
The Missing Spaghetti	978 1 84616 157 5
A Very Important Day	978 1 84616 154 4

All priced at £8.99

Orchard Colour Crunchies are available from all good bookshops,
or can be ordered direct from the publisher:
Orchard Books, PO BOX 29, Douglas IM99 1BQ
Credit card orders please telephone 01624 836000
or fax 01624 837033 or visit our website: www.orchardbooks.co.uk
or e-mail: bookshop@enterprise.net for details.

To order please quote title, author and ISBN
and your full name and address.
Cheques and postal orders should be made payable to 'Bookpost plc.'
Postage and packing is FREE within the UK
(overseas customers should add £2.00 per book).

Prices and availability are subject to change.